THE STORY OF CHALMERS OF NEW GUINEA

GET ALL OF THE 'HISTORY SHAPERS' BOOKS
The Story of...

David Livingstone	Robert Bruce	Chalmers of New
H. M. Stanley	General Gordon	Guinea
Abraham Lincoln	Lord Clive	Bishop Patteson
Sir Francis Drake	Captain Cook	Joan of Arc
Sir Walter Raleigh	Nelson	Napoleon
Columbus	Lord Roberts	Cromwell

PLEASE NOTE

In this series, you will read about historical figures who displayed courage, bravery, self-sacrifice, and many other admirable traits. Their stories remind us that many people in history took bold actions and made tough choices. Yet, even those who achieved great things sometimes held ideas or pursued goals that were not beneficial to everyone. History is full of complex individuals—parts of their lives inspire us to be brave and stand up for what is right, while other parts remind us to consider the unintended consequences of our actions.

As you explore these biographies, we invite you to reflect on the qualities that enabled these figures to achieve greatness and the lessons we can learn from their mistakes. Maybe you too can become a History Shaper—someone who learns from the past and helps to make our world a better place for everyone.

This edition published 2025
by Living Book Press
Copyright © Living Book Press, 2025

ISBN: 978-1-76153-569-7 (hardcover)
         978-1-76153-578-9 (softcover)

First published in 1906.

A catalogue record for this book is available from the National Library of Australia

THE STORY OF CHALMERS OF NEW GUINEA

by

JANET HARVEY KELMAN

TAMATE AND ROBERT LOUIS STEVENSON IN SAMOA

Contents

WHY THESE STORIES ARE TOLD

SEVENTY years ago a group of children gathered round a wise and kindly Scotchwoman, and ever, as one tale ended, they shouted, "Tell on, Bell, tell on."

Some of the stories she told are forgotten, and it is many days since the fortunes she read were proved true or false, but other little children re-echo the old request, and James Chalmers knew well how to answer it when he wrote for us of Kone and of Aveo, of the wild waves of the Pacific, and of the wilder men on its islands.

His life's adventure here is over. He will not come back to us nor tell us one tale more. But who shall say that we may not reach him one day, greet him with the old words, "Tell on, tell on," and listen, rapt and eager, to stories of brave deeds and strange voyages in that new world in which he lives?

BOYHOOD IN ARGYLL

JAMES CHALMERS was born sixty-five years ago at a little town in the West Highlands of Scotland. He was the son of a stonemason, but his home was close to the sea, and he was more eager to sail than to build.

One kind of building he did try. That was boat-building. But he and his little friends did not find it as easy as it looked, so they gave it up and tarred a herring-box instead. When it was ready James jumped into it for "first sail." His playmates on the beach towed him along by a rope. They were all enjoying the fun when the rope snapped, and the herring-box, with James in it, danced away out to sea. A cry was raised and a rush made for the shore. The fishermen were fond of the daring little fellow who was always in mischief. Soon they caught him and brought him safe to land. But they shook their heads when they saw how fearless he was. They knew he would soon be in some other danger.

When James was seven years old he left his first home and went to live in Glenaray, near Inveraray. Still the mountains of Argyll rose round his home. They were dim misty blue in summer, but in autumn and spring they were strong deep blue like the robes in stained-glass windows.

But the new home was not on the sea-shore. James could not tumble about in boats and herring-boxes all day long as he had done before.

Soon he found another kind of daring to fill his thoughts. From his home in Glenaray he and his sisters had three miles to walk to school. Other boys and girls crossed the moors from scattered farm-houses and crofts. A large number of children came from the town of Inveraray, and they gathered to them others whose homes lay between the town and the school. Here were two parties of young warriors ready to fight. James and the moorland groups were the glen party. The others were the town party. Some trifle started warfare. First there was a teasing word, then a divot of turf, and then before any one knew what had happened, stones were flying and fists pounding, and the clans were at war once more on the shores of Argyll.

The spirit of battle ran so high that on fighting days James and his sisters did not go straight home. They joined the larger number of the glen party and went round by the homes of the others, so that they had only the last little bit to go alone. There they were safe from the foe. But on days of truce they went with the town party to the bridges over the Aray. The Aray is a wild mountain stream, and when rain falls in the hills, it rushes wildly down and carries all before it.

One afternoon, when the sunshine had burst out after heavy rain, the children were going home together. As they came near the bridges the rush of the water and its noise drew them close to the banks of the stream.

James was there. He heard a cry: "Johnnie Minto has fallen in!"

He threw off his coat and gave a quick glance up the stream. There he saw Johnnie's head appear and disappear in the rush of the water. Without a moment's thought he slid down to the lower side of the bridge and caught his arm round one of its posts. Just above him Johnnie was tumbling down in the wild water. One quick clutch and James held him firmly. The water was so fierce and rapid that it seemed he must let go. He did let go, but it was the bridge that he lost hold of, not the boy! He let the current carry them both down till he could catch a branch that overhung the water. By it he pulled himself and his little foe (for Johnnie was of the town party) towards the edge of the stream till the other boys could reach them and drag them on to the bank.

Once James heard a letter read that had come from an island on the other side of the world. It told of the sorrows and cruelties that savages have to bear. He was touched. The stories of hardship made him wish to do and dare all that the writer of the letter had dared. The stories of sorrow made him long to help. He said to himself that he too would go when he became a man.

But soon he forgot all about that, and thought only of how much fun he could get as the days passed.

A BRANCH THAT OVERHUNG THE WATER

As he grew older he became very wild. He could not bear to meet any one who might urge him to live a better life.

He entered a lawyer's office, but the work did not interest him, and he filled his free time with all kinds of pranks, so that soon he was blamed for any mischief that was on foot in the town.

He was the leader of the wildest boys in Inveraray, but he himself was led only by his whims and the fancy of the moment. Until one day he found his own leader, who made work and play more interesting and delightful than they had ever been before.

James found that his life was not aimless any longer. It was full of one great wish—the wish to serve his hero, Jesus Christ.

Then he thought of his old longing to go and help those who were in pain and sorrow far away from Scotland.

It was not only because he was sorry for them, and because he wished to do the brave and daring things that others had done. These thoughts still drew him on. But far more than these, the love he had for his newly found Master made him wish to go.

He felt that it was a grand thing to be alive and young, and able to do something to bring to other lives the joy and strength that had come into his own.

Before he could go, however, he had to learn many things.

He went to stay at Cheshunt College, near London. The head of the college was a great man. It made it easier to be good to live beside him. Often afterwards, amongst hardships and dangers, his students thought of him, and of what he had said to them at Cheshunt, and were braver and stronger because of him.

While James Chalmers was at college, part of his work was to preach at a village eight miles away, and to go to see the people who were in trouble there. He was a big strong man, and enjoyed his walk of sixteen miles. Perhaps that was why this village, the farthest from the college, was placed under his care. The people there loved him, and to-day they still are glad to think that the "Apostle of New Guinea," as he was afterwards called, once preached and worked amongst them.

Mr. Chalmers could be solemn when he spoke of God and of life and death, and when he was with the villagers in times of sorrow and pain. But he still enjoyed all the glad things of life that he had loved in his boyhood, boating and swimming and fun of all kinds.

If he was in a restless mood when the others wished to study, the only way they could make him quiet was to give him charge of his part of the house. Then woe betide the man who made a noise. If some one else tried to keep order and he wished to romp, nothing would silence him.

One evening at supper time, as the students sat talking round the table, they heard a slow lumbering step in the passage. "Pad-sh, pad-sh," it came, nearer and nearer, till the door burst open, and a great grisly bear walked in on his hind legs. The men started up. The bear shuffled in amongst them. He grabbed a quiet timid student. Then the lights went out!

There was a great scrimmage. No one knew where the bear was, and no one could find matches. Even brave men did not wish to be caught in the dark by a runaway bear!

When at last the lights were lit, and they saw a man's face looking out from under the great head of the bear, they did not know whether to laugh more at him or at themselves.

They had been jumping here and there and dodging about, to get out of the way of James Chalmers in a bearskin!

The students were not the only people who were alarmed at the made-up bear. There was an Irishman who came to the college to sell fruit. One day, as he found his way along the halls, he met the bear. It was at the end of a passage, and they met so suddenly that the poor Irishman could save neither himself nor his basket from the paws of the great grisly creature.

THE GREAT GRISLY CREATURE

THE "JOHN WILLIAMS"

WHEN James Chalmers was twenty-four years of age, he and his wife left England for Australia in the *John Williams*. The lady he had married was eager to help in the great work that he had undertaken, so they were both very happy when they knew that they had really started on their long voyage. They enjoyed life on board ship and won many friends amongst the passengers and amongst the sailors.

The ship in which they sailed was new, and was one of the swiftest on the sea. She had been built with money given by hundreds of children, that she might take Mr. and Mrs. Chalmers and others who went to live as they did, from island to island on the Pacific sea.

They arrived safely at Sydney, in Australia, and from that town they sailed for the second part of their voyage.

The name of the island on which their first home was to be was Rarotonga. They could not go straight to it because others were on board, and the *John Williams* had to sail here and there amongst many islands. At one, two of her passengers must be left behind; at another, new voyagers must come on board; while here, there, and everywhere great bales of cargo must be landed. In these bales there

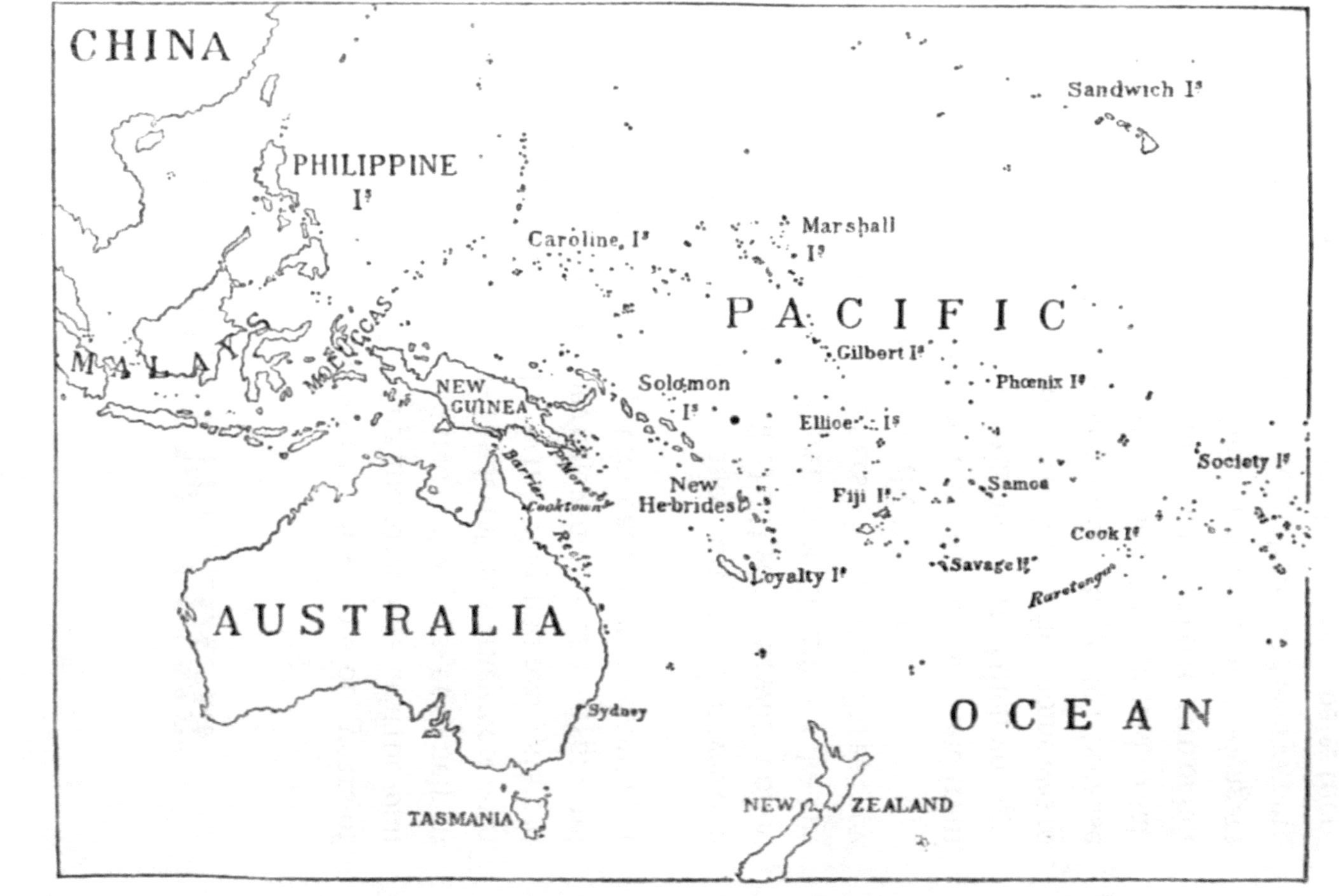

CHINA
Sandwich Is
PHILIPPINE Is
Caroline, Is
Marshall Is
MALAYS
MOLUCCAS
PACIFIC
Gilbert Is
NEW GUINEA
Solomon Is
Phœnix Is
Barrier Reef
Normanby
Cooktown
Ellice Is
New Hebrides
Fiji Is
Samoa
Society Is
AUSTRALIA
Cook Is
Savage Is
Rarotonga
Loyalty Is
Sydney
OCEAN
TASMANIA
NEW ZEALAND

were beads and knives, tomahawks and tobacco, and iron in bars, and rolls of cloth.

All these things were the money the white people used when they wished to buy food, or land, or boats, or houses from the people who lived in the islands.

It was very awkward to have to carry yards and yards of cloth instead of silver coins or bank notes! But bank notes and coins would have been of no useto the islanders; so the only way to do was to take to them what they wished, and the things the *John Williams* carried in her hold were the things they liked best.

Round many of the islands in the Pacific lie reefs. The reefs are built of coral by tiny insects, and they rise from a great depth almost to the surface of the water. The mingling colours of the coral are very wonderful when they are seen through the liquid blue and green of the waves.

But although these reefs are beautiful, they are very dangerous. If a ship runs upon one, the great waves quickly dash her to pieces as they break over her.

There are openings where the reef is broken for a short distance, or where its crest lies so far under the surface of the water that boats may safely enter the calm bays that lie within.

Very few ships had sailed in those seas fifty years ago. The captains had to guess where the reefs lay. Sometimes they sailed slowly, dropping a long line with a weight at the end of it, to find out if the ship had entered more shallow water. This is called "heaving the lead."

As the *John Williams* sailed near the first island at which she was to anchor, her passengers were watching the shore; they were delighted with the beauty of the island. It was a clear afternoon, and the rich land and trees offered a kind welcome to those who were to work there. Those who meant to go farther on to other islands, thought that if this first stopping-place were like the others, there would, for them too, be much to enjoy.

The reefs amongst which their vessel was sailing were beautiful, and their eyes were dazzled by the glisten and glimmer of colour under the water at the ship's side.

All at once those who were not standing very firmly on the deck were thrown down, and every one was trying not to believe the truth. But very soon no one could doubt it. Their beautiful ship had run on an unseen rock. She had all sail set and was going fast, so it was with a great crash that she struck.

Every one thought of what must be done to save the ship and her cargo. If they had had time to look round they would have seen hundreds of dark men running about the shore and hauling canoes to the water's edge. In a very short time the canoes were all round the ship, and the men were clambering up on deck.

Though they knew very little English, they all spoke at once, and they shook hands with every one. Then they began to help to work. It was a strange sight. Dark men and white all together hauled down the sails and launched the boats. Close to the reef, dark men dived into the water with blankets soaked in tar. They hoped to stop the holes the reef had made in the ship. White men gathered clothes and books and cargo together, and saw them put into the boats to be sent on shore. Through all the noise of boxes hauled along the decks and thrown out of the way, and high voices shouting questions and orders, came the steady thud of the pumps and the swish of the water as it poured back to the sea from the hold.

At high water the ship looked shattered, it is true, but when low tide came she looked ridiculous. Her stern went down as the tide fell, but her bows stuck fast high up on the reef. She looked like a great rocking-horse whose head has got so high that it cannot get down again.

So she rocked up and down twice a day with the tide, till at last, after all her cargo had been taken on shore, she was heaved off the reef into deep water. A great shout of joy rose as she slipped free.

But though she was free, she was greatly damaged, and had to go back to Sydney for repairs. She returned to the island nearly ten weeks later, as strong and sea-worthy as ever.

Then they sailed away again, first to the Loyalty Islands and then to Savage Island.

Mr. and Mrs. Chalmers saw how glad many of the natives were to welcome back their white friends. They saw, too, that the lives of men and women who had been savages had become noble and brave because white men who loved Jesus Christ had gone to live amongst them.

This made them long greatly to reach their own home and begin work there.

The ship was ready to sail from Savage Island. All the bales of cloth and the bars of iron that were to be left there had been put on shore. The cocoanuts and other gifts that the natives had brought had been taken to the ship. Every one hoped to sail for Samoa next morning. Mr. and Mrs. Chalmers went on board, while some of those who were to sail with them stayed on land for one night longer.

At night the wind fell and a great calm lay on every-thing. The *John Williams* lay out to sea, far beyond the reef, with her bow heading away from the island. The air was warm and the southern night seemed full of peace to all except the captain.

Though the ship had been lying waiting to set sail, she was not at anchor. No anchor could find holding-ground in the great depth of water.

The captain saw that his ship had been caught in a cur-rent, and that she was being carried steadily backwards to the island. Between the ship and the island lay the reef!

The *John Williams* had three boats. One after another they were launched and filled with rowers. Each boat carried a strong line with her. By these three lines the captain hoped the boats might hold the vessel against the current. The men were strong and eager to save their ship. They rowed to the seaward side of her and pulled hard at the oars. They toiled on and on till they were tired and aching, but still they lost way. Faster and faster the ship drifted towards the reef, dragging her boats after her.

Again they tried to anchor, but still no bottom could be found. Darkness fell deeper around them. Every sail was set in the hope that some breeze off the land might come in time. Blue lights were burnt on deck, that their friends on shore might know of their danger.

Thunder muttered. Flashes of lightning gleamed across the darkened sky. The white surf loomed nearer and nearer; the ship rose and fell on the backwash of the waves that broke on the reef.

Nothing could save her, but lives must be saved if possible. Seventy-two people were packed into the three boats, and very soon after the last one had left her side, the *John Williams* struck the reef.

Rain poured down on the open boats as they rowed sadly from the wreck. The landing-place was some miles away, and the surf was foaming wildly.

Earlier in the evening those on shore had caught sight of the blue lights. Some had run along the rocks to a point near the wreck. As they ran, the natives kept up a hooting cry that roused every one by the way. It was eerie to hear their call through the darkness and storm.

By the time the boats were trying to reach the shore, fires and torches burned brightly all round the bay to guide their rowers.

But no boat could reach the shore that night. The poor drenched voyagers had to leave their boats and get into canoes, then to leave the canoes and be carried by natives through the surf! In spite of all, they reached land safely.

But it was with sad hearts that they looked out across the bay at the wreck of their ship during the days that followed.

At last, in spite of many other delays, more than sixteen months after they had sailed from England, Mr. and Mrs. Chalmers reached the island of Rarotonga, where their home was now to be. The natives there knew a little English. As one of them carried Mr. Chalmers ashore he turned to him and asked:

"What fellow name belong you?"

"Chalmers."

Natives were crowding on the shore to see the stranger and to hear who he was. The man who carried him wished to be the first to find out and to tell the others. But the "Ch" and the "s" were too harsh for him to say, so instead of "Chalmers," he shouted, "Tamate!" And Mr. Chalmers was called "Tamate" to the end of his life. Mrs. Chalmers was called "Tamate Vaine," which was the native way of saying "the wife of Chalmers."

RAROTONGA

RAROTONGA is one of the fairest islands in the world. It has a white sandy beach; within that lies a belt of rich land. On this land, and even on the lower slopes of the mountains that tower one above the other in the centre of the island, banana trees, chestnuts, and cocoanut palms grow in clumps.

Tamate and Tamate Vaine quickly settled down to their work in Rarotonga. The life there was very quiet after the constant change and danger of the voyage.

The people who lived in Rarotonga called themselves Christians. They had given up fighting and the worship of the strange wild spirits whom their fathers had thought to be full of power. But though they had done this, many of them were still selfish and lazy.

Tamate would have liked to go at once amongst men who were much wilder, and who had never heard of the God who is love.

When he saw what his work in Rarotonga would be, he wrote to England to those who had sent him. He asked them to send some one else to Rarotonga, some one who would like to work quietly and to teach; and to let him go to a more dangerous place, where he could make it easier for others to follow him. But no one else could be sent then, and he could not leave his post.

When he found that he must stay in Rarotonga, he made up his mind that since he could not get the work he wished, he would throw all his strength into the work he had to do.

Part of it was to train native lads so that they might become teachers and go to other islands. Though they were men, he had to teach them a great many things that boys and girls learn at home when they are very little. He had to train them to be thrifty, and tidy too, because, when they went away to teach they would have to till their own gardens, and to grow their own crops, and to be at the head of a school without any one to guide them.

As Tamate spoke to the people in church Sunday after Sunday he wondered where all the young men were. There were old men and women, and young women and children, and there were his students, but he scarcely ever saw any other young men.

Where could they be?

He found that they spent their days, and often their nights too, in the thick tanglewood that is called "the bush," and that they drank orange beer there, and sometimes foreign drinks too. These revels made them useless for anything else.

The natives who knew Mr. Chalmers, and were beginning to love him, begged him not to go near the young men when they were drinking, because they were wild and fierce, and might kill him.

But Tamate never was afraid of any one. He went away alone, and plunged here and there through the bush, until he came upon a band of young men. Then he sat down and chatted with them. Very soon they liked him so much that though they would not give up drinking, yet they could forgive him when he knocked the bungs out of the beer barrels and let the beer run away. He was so brave and fearless that he could do this when the men were standing watching him.

Sometimes one or two of the young men gave up drinking, but Tamate wished to get hold of them all, not of one or two only, so he kept on winning their friendship, and waited.

His chance came. He heard that the young men were meeting to drill for war, and that they called themselves volunteers. This was startling. War had ceased on the island. No one was likely to attack them from over the sea. Why should they drill?

Tamate thought of the battles of Glenaray. He knew it would be useless to talk to these wild lads about peace and kindness, but he thought of another plan. He said to them:

"Why do you drill out of sight like this? Why not let every one see that you are 'Volunteers.' You must come to church, and sit together in the gallery."

The first Sunday after that a few of them came to church. The next week many more came, and from that time the Sunday Service became part of their drill. So eager were they to look well when they came to it, that they began to plant their lands that they might sell the fruit they grew, and buy clothes.

By-and-by the little church in Rarotonga needed a new platform and a new staircase. Then a great joy came to Tamate. He saw his young bushmen, whom he had first seen round their midnight fires, wild and fierce and useless, away out on the reefs cutting coral for the new staircase. They had learned to love the church and its services, and some of them became soldiers in the army of Jesus Christ.

When the church was ready to be opened again, there was great eagerness and stir. The natives had given nearly all that was needed. But there was still £25 worth of wood unpaid for.

Tamate was sure that the gifts that would be brought on the opening day would be worth much more than £25, but when he said so to a group of men, the doorkeeper said to him:

"How are you going to get in?"

"Why, by the door, of course."

"No, you will not. I have the keys, and I will not open the door until everything is paid. Of course you may try the windows."

Tamate was very glad that his doorkeeper cared so much about this debt. Though he had not meant to be so strict, he yielded to his friend.

CORAL FOR THE NEW STAIRCASE

But although the doorkeeper would let no one enter a church that was not paid for, he did not mean to keep any one out of church for a single day.

Soon a great noise was heard in the village. Boom went the drums. Boom! boom! High above their booming the voices of the villagers rose. Every one was called together to give what they could spare for the church. Very soon all was paid, and many gifts were left over.

All the time that Tamate was in Rarotonga he was longing to be at more dangerous work amongst those who lived to fight and kill each other, and who had no one to teach them.

His thoughts were so much with these wild tribes that he made others think of them too. Many of his students had caught his spirit, and longed, as he did, to go to the island of New Guinea, where very wild men lived and fought. Some of the teachers he had trained went before him. They knew it was dangerous, but they went with joy, because they too had learned how great and glad a thing it is to live for others.

At last Mr. Chalmers was allowed to leave Rarotonga and to go to New Guinea.

New Guinea is an island three times as large as Great Britain. It is very rich in fruits, in ebony wood, and in other things that traders like to find. It lies near to Australia. But the savages who lived in it were so fierce, and its rocky coast was so wild, that no one had tried to trade in the south-eastern end of it. Those who knew anything about it thought that to go there meant to die.

Four years before Tamate went to New Guinea, some of his teachers had landed at one of its villages, which was called Port Moresby. Here they found Mr. Lawes and his wife, who some months earlier had made their home there. They were the first white people who had lived amongst the natives of that wild coast. They found many tribes of natives, and each tribe was at war with the tribes around it. If two chiefs had a quarrel with each other, they brought their tribes to fight it out. Then the two tribes went on paying each other back in turn, till all their villages were burned and very many of their warriors were killed. Every one was either killing, or being killed, or afraid of being killed.

The men of New Guinea were large and strong, and they liked to look handsome. They thought it very handsome to have their hair standing far out on the tops of their heads and all round, with beautiful bright feathers stuck into it. They liked, too, to wear sticks like tusks through their noses, and rings through their ears, and necklaces of bones.

They daubed themselves all over with bright, sticky paint. But what they thought most handsome of all was to have a great many tattoo marks. When a man had killed another he was allowed to have his skin pricked with coloured dye. Afterwards the dye would never come out, no matter how hard the skin was scrubbed.

No one was allowed to have these coloured marks until he had killed a man. That was why the wild men of New Guinea were so proud of tattoo marks. Each mark proved that the man who bore it had been strong and clever.

It did not always prove that he had been brave, because sometimes the spear that had killed had been thrown from behind the foe.

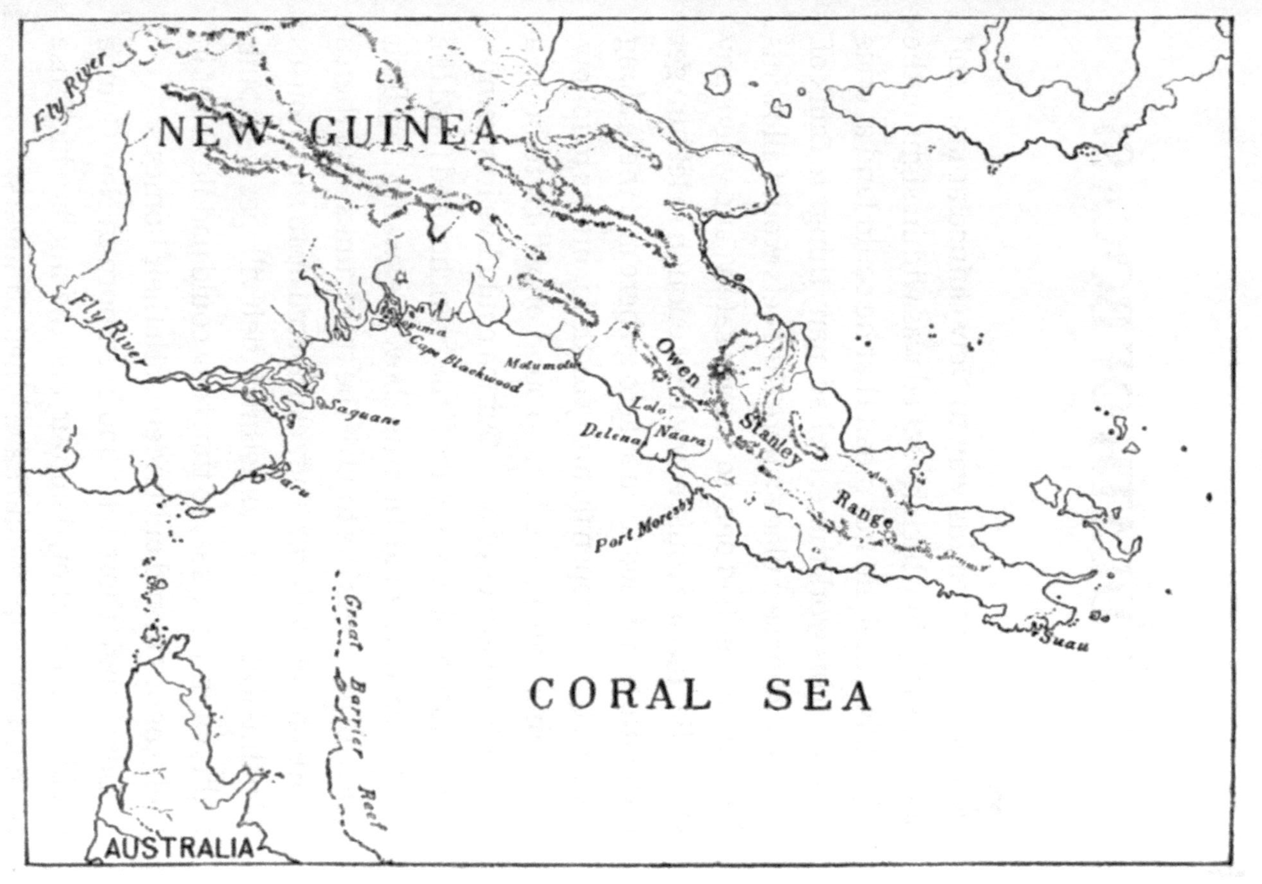

NEW GUINEA
Fly River
Fly River
Kapama
Cape Blackwood
Motumotu
Saguane
Daru
Owen
Lolo
Delena
Naara
Stanley
Range
Port Moresby
Suau
De
CORAL SEA
Great Barrier Reef
AUSTRALIA

THE DEATH OF BOCASI

TAMATE was on his way to New Guinea at last, and soon the ship in which he sailed was within sight of the island. But that did not mean that he could land at once and begin his work there. He had many things to think of. He must choose a place where the reefs would allow his boat, if he ever had one, to anchor safely; and where any ships that passed could come near enough to let him get on board. He wished to be able to go here and there along the coast, and to open up many roads for others to follow.

He must also have firm ground on which to build a house. The natives of New Guinea could live in swamps. They chose great trees, cut off the branches and fixed the stem deep in the mud. High up above the swamp they built a platform across the tops of the tree trunks, and then a house on the platform. They clambered up to their houses by palm-leaf ladders. Sometimes their villages were built right out into the sea, so that they could paddle about in their canoes in and out underneath their homes.

But though those who had been born in New Guinea could live so, the hot, damp air, and the smells which rose from the swamps would have killed strangers.

Besides that, Tamate wished to teach those he gathered

about him to grow many kinds of plants for food, so he had to choose a place where the soil was good.

After a long time he sighted the island of Suau, which looked as if it might be the right place. It lay close to the mainland.

In the bay beside it a single canoe paddled about. There was only one man in the canoe—a big, wild, cruel-looking native. He was fishing. Though he was fierce and strong, he was in terror when he saw the ship. His fishing was forgotten, and he paddled with all his might for the shore.

But the ship could sail much more quickly than his canoe, and soon she overtook him.

Tamate held up some bright beads and a piece of iron, and offered to give them to him, to show that he meant to be friends and not to hurt him in any way. The man waited to get the gifts, and then made off to the shore, while the ship anchored in the bay.

Very soon canoes came out to the vessel, and dark figures clambered up her sides and over her deck. They were very curious to know what kind of a thing this big "canoe" was, and to see the strange white people on board; and they wished to get beads and iron if they could!

Tamate Vaine sat knitting. And as the natives looked at everything and every one, they watched her too. She was the first to win a friend; for there was one big savage, called Kirikeu, who was so much charmed by her and by her knitting that he did not trouble to go with the others to see all that was in the boat, but sat still and watched her. They could not talk to each other at all; but when at sunset time he knew that he must go ashore, he made signs to her that he would go away and sleep, and that when morning came he would return with a gift for her. He could not tell her what the gift would be, but he showed her it would be something to eat.

By the time the sun began to rise next morning the canoes of Suau were ready to paddle to the ship again. Leading all the others was one in which Kirikeu sat with the food he had said he would bring.

But although Kirikeu was friendly, all the others were not. Many of them looked as if they would be glad to pick a quarrel. Their faces were frowning and angry.

Still, Tamate thought he would risk it. From a sailor who had picked up a good many of the words spoken on another island which lay near, he had learned all that he could. At many of the points at which he had landed to look for a home, he had used those words, but he found that no one knew them. The tribes in New Guinea speak many different languages. Here at Suau he found that the natives did know what he meant when he used the words the sailor had taught him. This made him more eager to stay. One other thing he must have. That was good water. A party from the ship landed. When Kirikeu knew that they were looking for water, he led them to a fresh stream.

Near the stream Tamate saw a piece of land that he liked. He bought it from the chief. Then he and his teachers began to build a house. The natives followed him into the woods, and he showed them which trees he wished, and gave them tomahawks with which to cleave the stems. They thought this great fun. They did not do what he wished, because they cared for him, nor because they meant to be friendly. They were just like boys with new knives, ready to cut anything. If they had not been a little afraid of the white man, they would have liked to kill him with the tomahawks, and so get all the cargo in the ship.

Tamate and his wife lived in one end of the chief's house until their own was built. They hired a room from him. It was a strange room. The bed was spread on the floor. It had no table, nor chair. A wall, only two feet high, ran between it and the room in which the chief lived. It was startling, on wakening in the dim light before the sun rose, to see bones and skulls glimmering from the roof, and dark figures passing through the room.

Houses do not take long to build when they are quite simple, and are made of tree stems and palm fronds. Soon the new house was firm and strong. There was very little in it, and the seats and tables and beds were bare and plain.

Tamate was eager to get all his beads and cloth into the house in order to let the little ship that still lay in the bay sail away. It was not easy to take this bulky money from the boat to the house. Whenever a native saw anything he wished to have, he thought he would like to get it at once, and asked for it. If it was not given to him, he grew angry, and perhaps he stole it when no one was at hand.

One afternoon a band of armed natives passed Tamate. They were daubed with war paint, and looked very terrible. They carried their spears and clubs as if they were ready to use them at any moment. In spite of the daubs of paint, Tamate knew that some of them were men who had been friendly with him. He shouted a greeting to them, but they frowned, and hurried on to the chief's house where the teachers were. He hastened after them, and went in amongst them. He found that they were led by a chief from the mainland, and that they wished gifts. The Suau chief round whose house they crowded, was very angry. He talked and shouted to the warriors from his platform. Then he called to the teachers to bring guns. When he saw that they would not do it, he rushed in and seized one himself.

Tamate tried to calm his friend, and to make him see that they would not fight, because they had come to bring peace to the island, not war.

The fierce-looking man whom they had seen first in his canoe in the bay, ran at Tamate with his club in the air.

"What do you want?"

"Tomahawks, knives, iron, beads; and if you do not give them to us we shall kill you!"

"You may kill us, but never a thing will you get from us."

He had to hold to his word alone. The teachers wished him to give the mainland chief and his people some little things for fear they would kill them all. But he said:

"Can't you see, if we give to these men, others will come from all round and ask gifts, and the end will be that we shall all be killed. No; if they mean to kill us, let them do it now, and be done with it!"

Then Kirikeu came, and begged him to give something. By this time this first Suau friend cared a great deal for the white man, and wished to help him. He thought it was the only way to get rid of the warriors. But Tamate said:

"No, my friend, I never give to people who carry arms."

Then Kirikeu and the Suau chief began to shout to the strangers again. At last the wild yells came more seldom, and the men from the mainland went with the men of Suau into the bush to talk out the quarrel. Once more they sent to ask for a gift, and once more they were answered as before:

"I never give to armed people."

Next morning Kirikeu brought the mainland chief to Tamate. Now the warrior was unarmed. The anger and fury of the night before were gone. When he found that he could not force the stranger to give him anything, and that Kirikeu and the Suau chief would not allow him to kill him, he thought that the best thing to do was to try to make peace, and this Tamate gladly did.

While the others were building, Mrs. Chalmers had been winning another friend. A bold young warrior, named Bocasi, used to sit beside her on the platform of the chief's house. He taught her to speak the Suau words, and she taught him to knit.

Many other natives were becoming friendly to the strangers. Sometimes they brought gifts of vegetables and fish, and sometimes they invited them to their feasts.

Tamate thought that he might leave his teachers in charge at Suau for a short time, and go, in the little ship that still lay in the bay, to see some other villages along the shore. He was very busy clearing out some "bush" near the house, that he might get it planted before he went, when one of the crew came to him, and said:

"I 'fraid, sir, our captain he too fast with natives. One big fellow he come on board, and he sit down below. Captain he tell him get up. He no get up. Captain he get sword, and he tell him if he no get up he cut head off! He get up; go ashore. I fear he no all right. Natives all look bad, and he been off trying to make row we fellow."

Tamate knew that the "big fellow" was Bocasi. He was vexed that he and the captain had quarrelled, but he did not think there was danger. He said to the sailor:

"Oh no; I think it is all right."

Then he told the men to stop work. As he was paying them, he heard two shots fired from the ship. He reached the house with a bound. The ship was a small one, not the one in which they had come to Suau, but another which had stayed beside them with cargo until they could land everything they needed. Its crew numbered only four, and this morning the captain and the cook had been left alone on board. The other two were on shore, helping to clear and to plant.

Whenever Tamate heard the shots, he sent these two sailors off to their captain. As he looked out to the ship, he saw natives swarming all over her deck, and some of them tugging at her anchor chain. On a point of rock that ran out towards the ship other dark figures crowded.

What could the captain be doing? Was he going to let the men in the canoes carry the line from his vessel to the wild crowd on the rocks, that they might pull the little ship ashore and wreck her?

Then a great noise rose from the beach, where the ship's boat lay, and the two sailors came running back to say that natives were in the boat, and would not let it go back to the ship.

Tamate ran off, leaping over fences and bushes till he reached the shore. He sprang to the boat. The natives fled before him, and soon the sailors were rowing hard to reach the ship.

When the natives on board saw them coming they took fright, slipped down into their canoes, and made for the shore. Those on the reef ran back to the village. When the sailors reached the ship, they found their captain lying on deck with a spear-head in his side, and gashes on his head and foot. They were so angry that they began to fire at the crowd of natives that surged backwards and forwards on the shore. Two men were wounded. Tamate did not know what to do first. He longed to get to the ship to stop the firing, but for the moment all he could do was to bandage the wounds of the two natives. Meanwhile the villagers were arming. Clubs and spears seemed to spring from the ground on every side. Angry voices asked, "Where is Bocasi?" "Where is Bocasi?"

Bocasi had gone to the ship and had not come back.

Mr. Chalmers asked two native men to take him in a canoe to the ship. He was very anxious to know what had kept Bocasi. He was too eager to wait till he was on board, so he shouted when he came near—

"Is there still a man on board?"

"Yes, he board."

Something about the voice of the man who answered made Tamate's heart sink. He cried, "Is he shot?"

"Yes, he shot dead. Yes, he dead!"

When he got on board he found the captain faint and white. Bocasi had tried to kill the captain, and the captain had shot Bocasi.

The captain might die of his wound. He must be sent to some place where he could be nursed. The body of Bocasi must be taken to Suau. The people there were angry already. When they saw the dead body they would be full of fury. If Tamate went back in the same canoe with it, they would kill him in their first burst of wrath. His wife and the teachers would be left at their mercy, and all his dreams of help for the men of New Guinea would be over. If he let the body go before him, his wife and the teachers would be slain, and he would not be allowed to land again.

One thing must be done first. By hook or by crook he must get ashore before the body. The canoe in which he had crossed lay alongside. The men were just going to place the body in it to row it to the shore.

"Stay," he cried; "wait for a larger canoe to carry Bocasi's body."

While they paused, he seized one native who was still in the canoe, and said, "Take me to shore quick, and give me time to reach the house before you land the body."

It was never easy to disobey Tamate, so before the other native had time to object, the little canoe was safely on its way to the shore.

Mr. Chalmers was grateful to reach his house and to be amongst the men of Suau again, but he knew that the hardest time was still before him.

When the dead body was brought to land there was great mourning and wailing. Bocasi was a warrior. He was young and handsome, and his people were proud of him.

The natives could not make up their minds what to do. Now they carried their weapons lowered for peace. Again they strutted about with them raised for war. East, and north, and west canoes could be seen. They were all coming to Suau. From each canoe as it touched the island a band of armed men landed, joined the crowd and added to the tumult. As the twilight fell, Tamate sent out bandages and medicine to the captain, and told him to be ready to sail that night.

A party of natives came rushing to the fence which ran round the bare new built house.

"Come out and fight," they shouted, "and we will kill you for Bocasi."

Then a chief came. "You must give payment for Bocasi's death," he said.

"Yes, I will give, but remember I have had nothing to do with Bocasi's death."

"You must give it now."

"I cannot. If you will come to-morrow when the big star rises I will give it you."

The chief went sulkily away.

Soon afterwards a native stole out of the bush. He did not speak angrily nor ask for gifts. He had come on another errand.

"Tamate," he said, "you must go to-night. At midnight you may have a chance. To-morrow morning when the big star rises they will kill you."

"Are you sure of it?"

"Yes, I have just come from the chief's house. That is what they have agreed. They will do nothing till to-morrow morning."

Tamate told this to his wife, and asked her if she wished to go away. Perhaps he knew what she would say. At any rate she answered as he would have done.

"We will stay. God will take care of us. If we die, we die: if we live, we live."

Then they asked the wives of the teachers. They were brave too. They said, "Let us live together or die together."

That night they gathered quietly for evening service

in their strange new home. They could not sing lest the sound should bring the natives to attack them. Though the teachers knew English, they were not quite at home in it, so Tamate spoke in Rarotongan, that they might follow every word.

On the hush, broken only by his voice in prayer, a grating sound fell. It was the clank of the chain, on the side of the ship and on the windlass, as the anchor was drawn up.

When they rose from prayer and looked out, the ship was leaving the bay. The last chance of escape was gone. They were alone amongst the fierce and angry natives.

Instead of going to sleep, Mr. and Mrs. Chalmers spent the night making parcels. They tied up large gifts for the near friends of Bocasi and smaller ones for the others.

Through the darkness came the sound of war-horns, and the shouts of bands of fighters who came from the other side of Suau and from the mainland. At four next morning the chief strode in. He looked at the gifts.

"It is not enough; can you not give more?"

"If you wait till the steamer comes I may."

"I must have more now."

"I cannot give you more now."

Groups of natives came to the fence. They shouted: "More, give more."

But no notice was taken and they went away. Daylight came, and still the new house and those within it were unhurt. Kirikeu wandered near the house.

"Let no one go out," he said.

The day passed slowly, but still he kept close to the house.

About three o'clock next morning Tamate lay down to rest. But scarcely had he fallen asleep when his wife roused him.

"Quick! They have taken the house."

The door was only a piece of cloth hung across the entrance. Tamate sprang to it and drew aside the curtain. In front of him a great band of armed men swayed. Another party blocked the end of the house. In the dim light the chief from the mainland stood out as leader.

"What do you want?" shouted Tamate.

"Give us more, or we will kill you and burn the house."

"Kill you may, but no more payment do I give. If we die we shall die fighting."

The chief cowered in fear. The weapon of the white man was uncanny and strange. The courage of the white man alone against them all was stranger still.

"Go!" said Tamate; "tell the others there must be an end of this. The first man who crosses the line where the fence stood is a dead man. Go!"

And they went! They went and talked. Talked wildly and fiercely too, but in less than two hours Kirikeu came to say that all was well.

On the shore they saw a large war-canoe ready to start, and watched the quick dark figures of the natives as they lifted hundreds of smaller canoes into the water. The warriors from the mainland shouted back: "We return to-morrow, to kill not only the white man and his friends, but to kill all of you." But before to-morrow came they thought they would stay at home!

The white man's courage had awed the natives, and though the chief of Suau would have liked to get larger presents, he did not wish the strangers to be killed. The iron and beads they brought had made him wealthy. When he saw that nothing would move Tamate, he turned against the others.

"If you try to kill him," he said, "you must kill me first."

That was why the mainland chief said he would kill the men of Suau with the strangers!

THE SPIRITS OF THE HEIGHT

IN time the natives grew friendly again. Then Tamate thought of other places. He had not come to New Guinea to teach and help the people of one little island on its shore only.

He wished to go here and there and everywhere, that far and wide he might let men know that he and those who followed him meant peace and friendship. So he would open the way. Later he would go back to leave teachers with the chiefs whose friendship he had won. In many villages his students would have been killed at once if they had gone alone. It needed a man of strong courage, quick wit, and great heart to go first. All these he had.

When he went away to make peace with new tribes he would have liked to take his wife with him, and she wished very much to go. But she was as eager as Tamate was to think of others first. She was a strong woman. She did not say much, but whenever she saw what was the right thing to do she did it. She knew that the teachers would be lonely if they both went, and that the natives might not be so willing to please them as they now were to please her husband and herself. So when Tamate went away she stayed at Suau.

It was very hard to say good-bye, because each of them knew that they might never meet again, and that either of them might need the other more than they had ever needed any one.

One time it was more hard than it had been before. Tamate wished to visit the village of Tepauri. The tribe who lived there were at war with Suau. In the last battle the people of Suau had killed a great many of the others. Tamate wished to make peace between the two tribes.

One afternoon he said: "I am going to Tepauri to-morrow; will you go with me?" Even Kirikeu refused to go with him.

That evening, as he and Mrs. Chalmers sat at their door, a troop of natives came to them. The dark men carried strange white things in their arms. When they came near they set them down in front of the house. They were skulls! Kirikeu spoke for the others. He said: "Friend, are you going over there to-morrow?"

"Yes, I mean to go."

"Do you see these skulls? They belonged to people we killed from over there. They have not been paid for. They will take your head in payment, for you are our great friend!"

He looked hard at Tamate and added: "Will you go now?"

"Yes, I will go to-morrow morning, and God will take care of us."

Beni, a Rarotongan teacher, was a widower. Tamate

said to him: "You heard all the natives said yesterday. I am going to Tepauri. Will you come?"

He agreed, and the two went off together. When they reached Tepauri they found themselves in the midst of a wild dancing mob. The natives shouted and waved their spears and their clubs, and made believe to throw them.

Every now and again they cried: "Goira, Goira."

This sounded like a Rarotongan word which meant "spear them." The natives caught Tamate's hand and rushed along the shore with him. The teacher was forced to follow close behind, and still the men of Tepauri danced and shouted and aimed their spears at unseen foes.

They came to the bed of a stream. Tamate stuck his heel against a stone to try to stop himself, but he was lifted over it and on and on, stumbling and running and clambering up the stony bed. He turned to Beni and said, "Try to get back. They may let you go."

"I am trying all the time."

"What do you think of it?"

"Oh, they are taking us to the sacred place to kill us!"

"It looks like it."

The thick undergrowth was so close and tangled that there was no hope of escape into it.

"No use," said Tamate. "God is with us, so let us go quietly."

From the dry stones of the stream bed and the thick bush, they came to a beautiful cool pool of water, hung round with ferns and moss. Then one of the men who had dragged them along made a speech. They did not know all the words then, but they could gather the meaning of the whole. This is part of it.

"Tamate, look, here is good water. It is yours and all this land is yours. Our young men will begin at once to build you a house. Go and bring your wife and leave these bad murdering people you are with, and come and live with us."

"Goira" was their word for water.

When Tamate and Beni returned to Suau the natives there could not believe that the people of Tepauri had not hurt them. They looked at them anxiously and said:

"They did not kill you, but did you eat anything there?"

"Oh yes, plenty."

"You should not have done that. They will have poisoned you."

When the natives of Suau saw that Tamate Vaine stayed alone with them when her husband went away, they were delighted. They said to each other:

"They trust us, we must treat them kindly. They cannot mean us harm, or Tamate would not have left his wife behind."

They used to beg her to eat a great deal, so that her husband would know that they had treated her well.

But the fever that seizes so many people there had weakened Mrs. Chalmers. Her spirit was so brave and strong that neither she nor any one else knew how ill she was.

Once Tamate went for a long walk on the mainland across the water from Suau. He wished to find out if it would be wise to send teachers far inland amongst the mountains. On this walk an old chief was leader of the party. They needed him to show them the way across the mountains, but the chief was eager to help in other ways that seemed to him more useful.

It was a bright sunny morning when they set out, and merry laughter and shouts rose from the travellers. Soon they came to a spot where a woman had died. The laughter died away. With solemn faces the chief and his men tore down branches from the trees and ran on brushing their feet with the branches, to keep the spirit of the dead woman from tripping them up. When they passed that bit of road, the run quieted down to a walk. Then rain began to fall. Again the chief took the care of the journey on his head. He scolded the rain and bade it be gone.

They spent the night in a little village. Tamate tried to sleep, but ever through his sleep he heard his guide's voice telling of the strange doings of the white man and of the great "war-canoe" that had called at Suau.

Next morning the chief gathered all the party together on an island in the midst of a stream. The way for the day lay uphill, but ere the climb began, the spirits that lived in the heights had to be made friendly. A great leaf was laid on the ground. An old cocoanut was scraped into it. Other leaves were cut into little pieces and mixed with the cocoanut, while the chief and five others sat on the ground and sang a low chant. Then they sprang up suddenly with a shout, and the natives squeezed some of the juices of the leaves and cocoanut over their heads. But this was not all. They waded into the stream and stood in deep water with their eyes gazing at the mountain-tops and their hands on their mouths. A low murmur reached the ears of those who watched them from the island. Suddenly another shout rose, and the sound of splashing water as the men plunged into the stream. The chief was the last to return to the island. Tamate asked him:

"Is it all right?"

"Yes, very good. The mountain spirits have gone, and the chief on the other side will be ready for us. We shall eat pigs. We shall put on armlets. And more food will be given to us than we shall know what to do with."

All the way up the chief was very solemn. He would pluck a leaf, talk to it, throw it away and pluck another. A bird on a twig before him was enough to bar the way. He bade it be gone, and stood motionless till he saw it fly.

The walk was a happy one, but Tamate felt that there were many other parts of New Guinea that were more in need of teachers, so he did not place any there then.

When he returned to Suau he found his wife very ill, and in a few months he had to let her sail away to Sydney. She could not get well at Suau, but they both hoped that rest and change in Australia would make her strong again.

He worked on at Suau, but the letters from Sydney brought him sad news. His wife was growing weaker

ANOTHER SHOUT ROSE

instead of stronger. A few months after she had left him a friend came to help him, and he gladly left this friend in charge at Suau and sailed for Sydney, but ere he reached his wife, he read in a newspaper that she was dead. She died amongst loving friends. She was bright and strong to the end, and her thoughts were full of others' needs. One of her last messages to her husband was:

"Do not leave the teachers."

Mr. Chalmers sailed back to New Guinea to find a new home and new work at Port Moresby.

KONE

PORT MORESBY is a village on the mainland of New Guinea. It lies to the north and west of the island of Suau. Here Mr. Chalmers made his new headquarters beside Mr. and Mrs. Lawes. Together they planned and began the working of a training-school that they might have New Guinean teachers.

Tamate used to say that to do Christ's work in New Guinea one was needed to break up the ground, another to sow, and another to reap. Although during his lifetime he saw many of the fierce men of the islands won for Christ, and trying to live as He wishes men to live, still the greater part of his work was to break down the hatred and cruelty of the wildest tribes. So, though he had his house at Port Moresby, he was seldom there for any length of time.

On one of his voyages westward along the coast he sighted three canoes. The men in the canoes were waiting to trade with natives from the village of Namoa. When they saw Tamate they all went ashore and ate together on the beach. Still there was no sign of the Namoans.

"Why not walk to Namoa?" said one.

"Why not?"

"And Tamate will come too!"

He did not wish to go. He was on his way to a village farther west. But the others were very eager to have him with them, and he yielded. As they started he looked round doubtfully.

"I fear it will rain before we can get back," he said.

"Not till we return," answered a native woman.

"Why not?"

"The rainmaker is with us, and he only can bring rain!"

"Where is he?"

The woman pointed to a chief named Kone.

"What about rain, Kone?"

"It cannot rain, so do not fear."

"But I think it will rain."

"You need not fear; let us start."

As they walked he said again:

"Kone, it will rain!"

"It will not," Kone said. Then he turned to the mountains and shouted:

"Rain, stay on the mountains! Rain, stay on the mountains!"

"No use, Kone; rain will come."

Soon the rain began to fall in torrents.

Kone thought that Tamate had brought the rain by stronger magic than he himself could use. He said:

"You are a great chief, and so am I, but the rain has listened to you."

"Come, my friend, I have told you of the great and good Spirit and of His power."

But Kone only laughed.

The kindly Namoans made the strangers welcome. They feasted them in their clubhouse till the rain was over and the stars shone on the white chief and the dark natives, who gazed with awe on the man who had brought rain in spite of Kone.

After this Mr. Chalmers often met the rainmaker, who loved to sit and listen while the white chief told of the fierce men who lived towards the sun-setting, and of the way in which he had brought peace amongst many of them. Kone offered to visit him at Port Moresby. Tamate was amused. He thought it was only in order to get tobacco and tomahawks and beads that Kone meant to come. Kone did wish to get these things, but the thought of peace had got into his mind, and he had begun to love his new friend greatly too.

Mr. Chalmers wished to place a teacher in the village of Delena, where Kone's home was. So he stayed there for some time to take charge of the building of a house and to prepare for a school.

One night he saw that all his friends in the village were excited. They feared an attack from the Lolo tribe, who lived near. Natives moved quickly hither and thither. Women glided past and were lost in the bush. They carried bundles. Soon they returned with empty hands. They had hid their treasures. Natives came to him. They whispered to him and pointed to his guns.

"Shoot, Tamate. Shoot for us, and frighten the Loloans and send them away."

In the simplest words he tried to tell them that he had not come to scatter people, but to gather all together. To bring peace; to change foes into friends.

The troubled natives did not know what he meant. To-night they spoke to this great white chief. To-morrow he and they might be lying dead, and yet he would not shoot!

They could not understand him, but sometimes a glimmer of what he wished flashed on them, and they turned away with a half hope that he would save them some other way if he would not save them by his gun.

On the night of the attack Tamate fell asleep. He was content to trust to the quick ears of his little terrier or the ready alarm of his boy. Beyond the tents great lights were burning, so that no one could steal up unseen.

At two in the morning the alarm came. On every side there was noise and clamour. Tamate's tent was high above the village. Women and children flocked to it. They tumbled over each other in their eagerness to get into safety and to save their pots and ornaments. In spite of all that Tamate had said, they still hoped that he would use his guns!

Bundles of arrows and spears were carried into the bush and left there in hiding, so that if a warrior had thrown his last spear he had only to dodge into the tanglewood and come out terrible as before! At last the fighting began.

The natives once more urged Tamate to shoot.

"Come down and fight," they shouted.

He left the women and children in the care of his boy, and hurried down to the village. He had no gun, no spears, no arrows. But he had no fear. He came straight up to the warriors and shouted: "Peace!"

Then the sharp twang of the bow-strings ceased, and the hiss of the spears and arrows came more seldom, till a hush fell over all.

Tamate asked one man after another to give up his arms. And they did. Kone was at his side, and whispered to him:

"Yonder is the Loloan chief."

Tamate had met this chief before and had not been able to win his friendship. He must try again! He went to him, and somehow or other the next thing that happened was that he and the warrior chief were walking arm-in-arm to the tents. It sounds very funny to read about, but it was very serious that morning.

The Loloan chief promised to stop the fighting, and Tamate let him return to his men. But very soon some of the villagers came rushing up, shouting, "They will kill Kone! They will kill Kone!"

Tamate ran into the fight again. Many more Loloans had come. They danced wildly round in their war paint. Clubs and spears rattled and whizzed on every side. One blow fell on his head, another on his hand. An old friend drew him to the edge of the fight. The Loloan chief came to him.

"We will not hurt you; let us fight it out," the chief begged.

"No, no; you must stop, and see that you do not hurt my friend Kone."

When quiet came at last, Mr. Chalmers told them all, that he could not stay with them if they fought so, and that if they wished to have him there, they must not kill each other.

After the Loloans were gone, the men of Delena gathered round him to thank him.

"If you had not been here," they said, "many of us would have been dead, and the others away from their homes for ever."

While Tamate stayed at Delena, he had a short service each day at sunrise, and another at sunset. At first the natives came to see what the strange white man did. Afterwards they began to care for what he said. They found that this strong chief, who had brought rain when they did not wish it, and peace when they did wish it, cared very much about the words he spoke at sunrise and at sunset. They could see it. His face glowed. The man who had been calm when the arrows flew about him, grew excited when he spoke of his Master Jesus Christ. So they wondered and listened. But Kone waited when the others went away. He wished to know more. Tamate taught him a prayer: "Great Spirit of Love, give me light! Lead me to Christ, for Jesus' sake."

It is very simple, but it was not easy for Kone to learn it. Every now and then a smile came to Tamate's lips. He saw the rainmaker on his way from the village. He knew why he was coming and what he would say.

"Tamate, I have forgotten it."

Then he learned it again, and went off gladly, only to come back in a little while and say, "I have forgotten it, Tamate."

But before the house was built Kone had learned that prayer, so that he could never forget it.

Not long after Mr. Chalmers left Delena a great feast was held there. Kone's heart was full of love to his white friend who had saved him from death and had brought peace because he knew the great Spirit of Love. Kone, too, wished to bring peace. He would help Tamate's work and end the strife between the Loloans and the Naara tribe with whom they were at war. He thought the feast would be a good time to begin, so he asked two Naara men to come to Delena for it.

As the dancing began, he saw a Loloan steal up behind one of his Naara friends. The Loloan's spear was aimed at the stranger. There was no time for Kone to save his guest except in one way. He leapt in front of his friend, and the spear that was meant for the Naara man entered his own breast. He was carried home to die.

"Send for Tamate," he said, "send for Tamate." But

across the reef and up against the shore a great south-east wind was blowing, and no canoe could face the wildness of the sea.

In the darkness of pain and weakness, Kone could not have the joy of seeing his friend once more. But still in the shadow of death he sought for Tamate's Master, and murmured the words he had learned so slowly: "Great Spirit of Love, give me light! Lead me to Christ."

A few months later, Mr. Chalmers came back to Delena. He wished to go still farther west, and meant to take Kone with him. Kone was a good fellow-traveller. He could speak many languages, he was loved by the natives, and he was a constant joy to Tamate. The great childlike heart of the savage chief was like his own.

When the boat reached Delena, a canoe came out to meet her. But there were no shouts of welcome, and Kone was not there.

A chief stepped on board in silence, and at first would give no answer to the eager question, "Where is Kone?" Then he said, "Oh, Tamate, your friend Kone is dead."

"Dead?"

"Yes, Kone is dead, and we buried him at your house. The house of his one great friend!"

THE SPEAR ENTERED HIS OWN BREAST

THE BERITANI WAR-CANOES

"TAMATE" was the name by which the Rarotongans called Mr. Chalmers when he first reached the island. The natives of New Guinea called the British men-of-war "Beritani war-canoes." While Mr. Chalmers was at Port Moresby five of them came to New Guinea, and sailed about in its waters. Up till this time the south-eastern part of the island had always been left in the hands of the natives. If these men had been as able to keep away other people as they were to kill each other, it might have been left to them always. But although they were very clever with their bows and spears, they could do little against men who fought them with guns.

Mr. Chalmers and Mr. Lawes, and those like them, were not the only foreigners who came to New Guinea. Some very cruel men came. They wished to make a great deal of money, and they did not care how much they hurt other people in order to make it.

When they came to the island they bought land as Tamate did, but they did not pay for it as he had done. Sometimes they bought a large piece of ground, and gave the worth of one penny for it. The natives did not know what their land was worth, so they were willing to let it go for almost nothing. The strangers did not always take trouble to find out who really owned the land. They bought it from those who had no right to sell it.

But they did a very much more cruel thing than that. They tempted the natives to go away with them to work and to get many things they wished in payment for the work. The traders made the natives think they meant to bring them back in "three moons." Some of the men of New Guinea thought it would be nice to come home rich men in so short a time, and went with them. But three months, and six months, and a year passed, and still they did not return. Their friends at last mourned for them as dead, and gave the things that had been theirs to others. Often the natives were so angry, when they found out what had been done, that they killed other white men who did not wish to harm them.

Tamate had been in New Guinea for some years. By his kindness to the natives, he had made it more possible for strangers to trade there. But many sad things were happening. White men were cruel to natives, and natives were cruel to white men. Often both white men and dark killed people who had not hurt them, because they hated the whole race for what single men of it had done.

Every one who knew about it felt that this must not go on, and England sent her men-of-war to take Southern New Guinea under her care. She did not take it for her own. She only said that she would try to keep people from doing very wicked things there, and that she would punish those who were unjust and cruel to others, whether they were natives of New Guinea or not.

But the officers on board the men-of-war did not know the languages of New Guinea. They could not tell the natives why they were there nor what they wished to do. They asked Mr. Chalmers and Mr. Lawes to go with them to let the natives know why it was that the "Beritani war-canoes" had sailed to New Guinea.

One day all the chiefs that could be brought together from the tribes near, met on board the war-ship *Nelson* in the bay outside of Port Moresby. They feasted there together, and then returned to the village. But the doings of the day were not over. Two of the big guns began to fire, and the natives danced with surprise. When darkness fell, search-lights gleamed and glanced round the bay. They fell on the far-off mountains and on the palm groves, and lighted up each creek and cranny on the shore. They fell on the quaint houses of Port Moresby, and on the dark faces of the startled natives. Then came the shriek of the syren. It leapt about like an uncanny thing, and seemed to come now from the plashing waves and now from the depths of the forest. Dogs and men fled alike from the noise of it into the darkest corners of their homes. Then the quiet of night fell on the village and on the "Beritani war-canoes."

Next morning the officers of H.M.S. *Nelson* landed and marched to Mr. Lawes' house. Hundreds of black eyes watched them, and hundreds of ears listened with delight to the music of the band.

The Union Jack was hoisted close to the house. After that Commodore Erskine read a paper, which told what Britain would do for New Guinea, and what she wished New Guinea to do for her.

The chiefs did not know what the Commodore read, but Mr. Lawes said it all over to them in their own language.

Though Commodore Erskine was there in order to tell the men of New Guinea what Britain wished, he could not be long with Mr. Chalmers and Mr. Lawes without caring about their work too.

One afternoon, when his ship was in the bay, he came ashore to see the school. The village bell began to ring. It did not hang in a church tower, nor over the door of the school, but from the branch of a tree. One hundred and twenty boys and girls pattered into a long cool room. The walls and roof were made of plaited palm leaves, and the air could get in while the hot sunshine had to stay out-side. The children answered many questions. They knew where their own home lay on the map, and they thought of other places as near it, or far from it, for New Guinea was the centre of the world to them.

They sang "Auld Lang Syne," and "God Save the Queen," and afterwards they bowed their heads, and said, "Our Father which art in heaven." They did not say it in words that Commodore Erskine knew, but with reverence and trust which are the same all over the world.

The Commodore would have liked to give the children sweets and chocolates, but he gave them something that they liked much better. Each of them bounded away with a string of beads, a bit of tobacco, and a fish-hook!

At many other villages in New Guinea the people were told why the "Beritani war-canoes" had come to their shores, and why the Union Jack was hoisted.

At one place there was great joy because one of the war-ships brought back seventeen men who had been tempted away by traders. One was a chief, an older man than most of those who had gone. He sat gazing from the ship while a canoe came from the shore. The two men in it climbed up into the ship. Then there was a rush and a cry, and the three natives were together. One of the men in the boat was the brother of the old chief. He had thought he would never see him again, and now they were together, weeping and rubbing noses, which was their way of kissing.

But although the villagers were glad to see their friends again, some were full of sorrow. Many had gone away and only seventeen had been brought back. They gathered round Tamate and said:

"Where are the other boys? You have brought joy to some homes, but others are left in sorrow."

Mr. Chalmers wished them to go with him on the war-ship to tell Commodore Erskine of their friends. The *Nelson*, on which the Commodore sailed, was then at another part of the island. But the natives were far too frightened to go. One, who had a son away, was willing to give anything he had if the ships would only go quickly to bring back his boy.

"Now go to-day, and we will fill the ship with pigs," he said.

"Well, come and see the Commodore and tell him you want your son back."

"No! white fellow speak three moons, no bring him again. You go bring fellow boy back."

The screw gave a sudden turn. The native darted overboard into his canoe. He thought he was going to be carried off by force. When he saw the water rippling between his canoe and the great war-ship, he shouted:

"Bring boy back!"

TAMATE AND ANOTHER

AFTER this Mr. Chalmers went to England. While he was there he met the lady who afterwards became his wife. With this second Tamate Vaine he made a home at Motu-motu, the village of islands, a place still farther west and nearer the country of the wildest tribes of New Guinea.

Mrs. Chalmers entered into her husband's work with great spirit. She soon loved the wild villagers, and the chiefs from the country round her home. And the little dark-skinned children were a joy to her. But the climate told on her health, and her husband sailed with her to Sydney that the voyage and rest might strengthen her.

At this time there was another great Scotchman on an island in the Pacific. He, too, was trying to help those amongst whom he lived, though not in the same ways that Tamate helped. His name was Robert Louis Stevenson. He wrote delightful stories and poems, "Treasure Island" and "Kidnapped"; "Leerie" and "The Land of Counterpane," and very many more.

When he was a full-grown man he enjoyed romping just as much as Mr. Chalmers had enjoyed being a bear in Cheshunt College. These two men were like each other in many ways, and when they met on board the steamer from Sydney to the islands, they became friends at once.

There was a little smoking-room on board ship, and night after night the dim air was full of pictures, pictures of shipwrecks and strange weird places, of wild men in battle, and little children. They were the pictures that rose as one story followed another.

Too soon the steamer reached Samoa, where Mr. Stevenson's home was. The friends had not to part at once. Tamate stayed some days in the island, but he was so busy seeing people and speaking that there was not much time for story-telling. Twenty-four years before this, after the ship-wreck at Savage Island, he had landed at Samoa with nothing except the clothes he wore. He had made friends there as he always did, and now many of them, as well as others who had only heard of him before, wished to see him.

A great open-air meeting was held. Hundreds and hundreds of native men and women gathered to listen to him and to their own King Malietoa.

The white people who lived there wished to hear him too. They asked him to lecture to them. This he did, and Robert Louis Stevenson was in the chair at the meeting.

When Tamate sailed away from Samoa he hoped soon to see his new friend, but they could never meet again. The letters they wrote to each other were full of love and honour. In one of them Mr. Stevenson said:

"O Tamate, if I had met you when I was a boy, how different my life would have been!"

It was not only the wild men of New Guinea who loved Mr. Chalmers. Wherever he went he drew out all that was finest in men and women, and made them better and gladder because he was there.

When he and his wife reached Motu-motu the sea was very rough and they could scarcely land. But they were so eager to be amongst their friends there again, that they would not wait for calm. The little landing-boat lay alongside, but far down below the deck, and she danced on the waves like a cork. It was too wild to think of a ladder, so Mrs. Chalmers called out:

"Stand ready to catch hold of me, boys, and when she rises again, I'll spring."

Her husband said:

"That's the only way; but I fear you won't do it in time."

But before he had finished speaking Tamate Vaine found herself safely in the boat, not very sure how she had got there, but glad to be one step nearer home.

What a greeting met them. Every one was at the water's edge to welcome them home. The houseboys came as far out as they could on a bank of sand and ran alongside as the boat came in, and the dogs plashed into the water in their delight.

THE CHARMS OF AVEO

BY this time Tamate and Tamate Vaine had friends in hundreds of homes in New Guinea. The teachers from Rarotonga had grown into strong, good men and women. Their love for Tamate was like the love of children to a father. The little girls and boys at the village schools rushed to welcome the great white chief and his wife, and shrieked with laughter when they tried to speak the strange words of new tribes.

Many natives too had learned to love Tamate's Master. All life was changed for them because Tamate had come to New Guinea, and they felt for him a love that was deeper and stronger than their love for life. Often they went with him when they thought it was to death.

But Tamate had other friends, men who thought they knew better than he did, and who still worshipped cruel spirits as their fathers had done. Very many of them were true friends to Tamate, and found a big place in his heart and life. He loved them for their own sakes, and he loved them because he hoped that one day they too would love his Master.

When Tamate left Motu-motu, Aveo was one of these

friends. He lived at a very wild place farther west than Motu-motu.

Aveo was a great chief, but he seemed much more than a chief to the people who knew him. He had charms, and they thought that the strange spirit they feared was in him, and that he could make famines and storms and earthquakes. They feared that he would use his charms against them unless they gave him many gifts. When their canoes were lying deep in the water laden with sago, and they were ready to sail away, they gave arm shells and pigs to him and asked him to give them calm weather!

Tamate's first visit to Aveo was a strange one. He had heard much about the charms, and he wished to see them. Aveo had seen him before and was eager to welcome him. He made a feast. While the food was being cooked they sat and talked. Tamate asked about the charms. He found that Aveo believed in them himself as thoroughly as other natives did.

"Let me see those charms, Aveo."

"Tamate," said Aveo, "you are now my friend. If I showed you these things you would die. No one but myself must see them."

"Aveo, there is no chance of my dying or even being sick by seeing your things."

"Never, my friend Tamate, never."

"It is all right, Aveo, they can do me no harm."

A native who was listening said, "You may let him see

them. They will not hurt him. He goes everywhere and sees everything, and he is all right."

Aveo sighed and looked strangely at Tamate. Then he said, "I am afraid, but I will think about it."

At night Tamate lay down to sleep. His hammock was slung on the platform of a village house. He was very tired, but when he lay down he could not sleep. The night was hot and the air heavy. Strange noises rose to his ears from the other houses of the village and from the wild bush all round. About midnight another noise sounded through those vague ones. It was the sound of the fall of a naked foot on the palm fronds of the platform. It came nearer and nearer. Then a hand touched him and a voice whispered:

"Are you asleep?"

"No, I am not. Is it you, Aveo?"

"Yes, do you really wish to see those things?"

"Yes, I do."

"Are you sure they won't kill you? Will you not get sick and then die after you have seen them?"

"No, certainly not."

"I am afraid, greatly afraid, but come with me!"

Tamate slipped from his hammock and followed Aveo in and out through the village, till they came to the last house. It was built on the ground, not on stilts like the other houses. Aveo led the way, first through one room, then through another, till they came to a very small room in which a low fire burned.

When they were both inside it, Aveo put up a door across the opening by which they had entered, so that no one could see into the room. Then he piled wood on the flickering fire and soon the flames flashed up and lighted the dark corners and the two dim figures.

Then Aveo fetched a netted bag. It was small and dirty, but he handled it with great care. He opened the bag a little. Then he stopped.

"That must be enough, Tamate. You will die if I go on, and what then will I do?"

"No, Aveo, I will not die, so do not fear."

Then Aveo took out a parcel. It was bound up with fibres of cocoanut and native cloth made of bark. Tamate watched and watched. He began to think there was nothing except string and cloth. The logs were smouldering and everything was dim again. Tamate stirred the fire. A blaze lit up the room. Aveo stopped unwinding the fibre, and looked at Tamate. He could not see him well, for his eyes were full of tears, and tears were on his cheeks. His hands shook as he held the little parcel. He faltered, "O Tamate, you will die."

"No, Aveo, no; I am all right. Go on."

Then the last bit of cloth was unrolled, and Aveo put three little pieces of wood on the mat. The light from the logs fell on them. They looked like two little dolls and a tiny club. They were very old. Only one man could use them at a time. Long, long ago a father had given them to his son. He had told his son that his father had given them to him. Then the son had given them to his son. No one knew how old they were. No one had heard of a time when they had not been handed down from a father to a son. No one living had seen them except Aveo and Tamate.

Tamate wished to buy them, but Aveo would not sell them. He put them carefully away again. Then Tamate said to him, "Some day a man will come to live in your village. He will tell you of the God who made all things, and who loves us. After that you will not want these things any more. Promise that you will not sell them except to me."

Aveo smiled, for he was sure he would always wish to keep his charms. He said, "Yes, should it ever happen! I will give these things to my son when I have taught him all."

Then Tamate found his way back to his hammock and fell asleep.

Aveo came to him another night. This time he brought his sleeping-mat with him. His white friend was going away next morning, and Aveo wished to sleep beside him, or rather to stay beside him, for he did not try to sleep. He talked eagerly of a voyage he had made to Motu-motu and of the kindness that Mr. and Mrs. Lawes had shown him. All at once he stopped and began to sing to himself sadly.

Tamate said, "Aveo, what are you doing? Why have you left off your story so suddenly?"

Aveo pointed to the north. "When I see those two stars," he said, "I always do this. My father taught me. I know the spirit of the sea hears me. May I go on?"

"Yes, go on."

After the song was over, Aveo told Tamate about the spirits of the earth and the sea and the sky, till morning came.

When Tamate left Motu-motu to go far west to the wildest tribes of all, who lived near the Fly River, Aveo still trusted in his charms and in his songs to the spirits of the earth and sky and sea.

Many years afterwards, Tamate came back from the Fly River to see his old friends and to cheer the teachers who lived in the villages along the shore. When he reached the village where Aveo lived, the news of his coming spread quickly, and Aveo hurried to the teacher's house to see his old friend. After they had greeted each other, Aveo said, "What about those things, Tamate?"

"What things?"

"Why, have you forgotten them?"

Then suddenly the white man remembered the night he had spent in Aveo's village long ago, and the magic charms he had seen there.

"I remember them well," he said; "what of them?"

"Do you want them now?"

"Yes; will you sell them to me?"

"No—no payment, Tamate. At night when no one is about I will bring them to you."

At night Aveo came creeping in. He peered all round. He saw two men looking in at a door. They had been watching

Tamate as he wrote. Aveo wished no one to see. He said, "Send these men away."

When he saw that all the windows and doors were shut, he opened his bag and unwound the parcel as before. It was not so eerie as it had been in his own little room, with the gleaming logs.

Although Aveo no longer used his charms it was not easy for him to part with them, and Tamate was so much afraid that he would be sorry and ask them back again, that whenever he got the bag with its strange little dolls, he hurried down to his ship that lay at anchor near the shore. He could talk more happily with Aveo, when he knew that the charms were safely locked up on board.

Next morning Mr. Chalmers set sail for another village. There was a heavy sea rolling, and the little ship was driven against a point of rock. Although Aveo had tried to hide his charms from every one when he took them to Tamate, the natives had found out that they were on board. Though many of these men loved Jesus Christ, they could scarcely believe that the charms had no power at all. When the ship struck the reef they said, "Tamate has Aveo's things, and the ship is wrecked and Tamate drowned."

But in spite of the stormy seas every one reached land safely. The ship was floated off the reef and mended, and in a day or two Tamate and the charms sailed away out of the bay.

THE BARRIER REEF

BEFORE Tamate left Motu-motu for the Fly River he went to Australia. The *Harrier*—a little ship that took them from village to village in New Guinea—was broken and battered by the wild waves that surged on the shores of the island. But she had become so useful that the workers in New Guinea could not do without something in her stead while she was in dock under repair. Mr. Chalmers went to get another boat to do her work.

The *Harrier* crossed safely from New Guinea to the coast of Australia through stormy seas. She came to the great Barrier Reef that lies along the shore of that part of Australia. At some parts the reef is more than fifty miles out to sea, at others it runs almost close to the rocks of the shore. It has openings through which ships may enter the deep water within it. The *Harrier* made for one of these some distance north of Cooktown and entered it safely.

Although the night was stormy, and the wind against them, the crew were in great spirits, and sang "Homeward Bound" as they worked. They thought of their wives and the other friends who would welcome them in port. It was Thursday evening, and now that they were safe within the Barrier Reef they hoped to enter the harbour next morning.

But the weather was against them. Though they carried sail all night, they found when morning came that they were very little farther south than they had been the night before. They could not sail straight into Cooktown. They had to tack backwards and forwards between the shore and the reef. The wind was so strong that it carried away some of the *Harrier's* sails. The anchor was let go beside Three Islands, and the ship lay there till repairs were finished.

At four o'clock on Friday afternoon she set sail again. In the evening the captain began to hope that if he tacked once more out towards the reef he might bring her into Cooktown harbour with the return tack.

Tamate was in bed and half asleep. He heard the captain come down and go to the chart-room. Could there be any danger? He was too sleepy to trouble about that. A few minutes afterwards he was dreaming of striking a rock—bump, thump, scrape!

But was he dreaming? He started up wide-awake. In a minute he was dressed and on deck.

All hands were at work. The sails were hauled down. Then the ship's boat was launched. She carried an anchor out to deep water. As soon as it held, the sailors turned the windlass with all their strength. They hoped to heave the *Harrier* off the rocks; but no, she was firm. All night long each wave drove her against the reef. As the tide fell she leaned over to one side more and more till her crew could scarcely move from place to place on her deck. There was much work to do. They had to drag on deck all the heavy things that were on board, so that if she righted again with the evening tide they might throw them into the sea. They hoped that if she was as light as possible they might heave her off into deep water again.

All day long on Saturday they made signals of distress. But the hours wore on and there was no sign of help. They were out of the channel in which ships sailed for Cooktown.

The ship righted with the evening tide. Over went everything of iron and all heavy cargo into the sea. The men at the windlass worked till it seemed that the anchor-hawser would break. But the *Harrier* was too firmly fixed; she would not move.

The sea was still wild on Sunday morning. No one knew if the ship's boat could live in it. Yet if the boat did not go to seek for help, no one might see them and then they would all be drowned. They could not tell whether it was more dangerous to go in the boat or to stay on the ship. The *Harrier* was over on her side again. Before the boat was sent off the sailors slid and scrambled along the sloping deck and cut the stays. Then the masts were sawn partly through on the side of the ship that was upper-most. Every one climbed to the high edge of the deck, away from all the ropes and rigging, and waited. A great wave came. Crack, crack, went the masts, and away into the sea went masts and rigging that the ship might have a better chance of holding together till help could come.

Then the boat was manned. It was not easy to get into her down the side of the *Harrier*, whilst the waves dashed her wildly hither and thither.

"What are you doing?" shouted Tamate, still on the deck of the *Harrier*, to a sailor who was diving down to the hold searching for something.

"Looking for the poor old cat, sir."

He found him, too, and puss was dropped through the spray into the boat.

Then Tamate found another pet, a young cockatoo, half dead with fear, and screeching at the pitch of his voice.

"What about 'cockie'?" he said.

"Oh, we save him. He go in boat!"

So the boat with her strange crew rowed away. After fighting with the waves for two hours she reached the Three Islands. On one of the islands they found some empty huts that had been used by divers. There they lit a fire. Then they set fire to a patch of long grass on the island, in the hope that some passing ship might see the blaze.

The cat and the cockatoo were very funny. Puss had been so long at sea that he hated the dry land as much as most cats hate water. He was brought to land, but at each step on the sand he lifted his paw and shook it, and then suddenly he darted back through the shallow water and scrambled into the boat!

PUSS WAS DROPPED INTO THE BOAT

"Cockie" was miserable. He stood helplessly where he was set, and called for one of the sailors, his special friend. When he was taken to the fire he soon cheered up, but he would not stay alone even beside the fire. He looked very comical, with his draggled feathers, as he followed the sailors and scolded them if they left him.

On Monday morning a ship came near. She picked up those on the island and then steamed for the wreck. Even after she got close to it, it took hours to fetch all those still on board the *Harrier* from her to the steamer.

When at last they steamed away towards Cooktown, even the sadness they felt for the loss of their ship was forgotten for a little as they saw the harbour ahead of them and knew that they were safe.

THE FLY RIVER

AFTER Mr. Chalmers returned from this voyage, he and his wife went away to the mouth of the Fly River. The men of the wild tribes who lived there were not nearly so lovable as the savages of Motu-motu, and Mrs. Chalmers found it difficult to care as much for the ugly cruel children of the island of Saguane, where their home now was, as she had done for the children at Motu-motu.

Many new plans were in Tamate's mind. It was not enough for him that schools and churches were rising throughout New Guinea; that war was ceasing; that, when he landed at scattered villages, men and women were waiting his coming, to say openly to all, that they meant to follow Jesus Christ. He always wanted more. As long as those wild tribes of the Fly River fought and hated each other he could not rest. He wished to do more for them than to bring peace amongst them. He hoped that some of the men of those tribes at the mouth of the river, who had learned to love his Master, would go to live inland amongst the swamps and marshes, where even his Raro-tongan teachers could not live. So he began to train a band of these natives, as he had trained the men of Rarotonga and Port Moresby before.

In the midst of all his plans his wife grew very ill. He nursed her for three months, but her strength sank. The sea was washing away the shore of the island of Saguane where they lived, and they found they must leave it. They went to Daru, a village on the mainland, but Mrs. Chalmers only lived one day there. She had been very eager to reach this new home, which was to be her last on earth. Her wish came true. She was buried in the native graveyard, and her husband was left once more to work in loneliness.

He did not lose courage. He threw himself more keenly than ever into his work. But his own strength was failing, and he found it harder to go long journeys without rest. Sometimes he thought he was growing lazy when he felt that he was not able to do as much as he had once done.

One morning he set sail on the *Nieu*, which had taken the place of the *Harrier*, for Cape Blackwood. The natives there, and on the large island near, were very strong and fierce. Tamate knew that he might be killed, but then he knew, too, that if he could win those wild men, he would take away the great barrier between Christ and the tribes who lived round the gulf of water into which the Fly River flowed. If these men were to stop fighting and to listen to the story of Christ, other tribes would be glad to do so too. They would be grateful to be free from the fear of these cruel warriors.

It did not matter much to Tamate whether it was by his life or by his death that he won them. Either way he must break down the wall that shut out the joy of life from so many people.

There was a young friend who had come to New Guinea with the same hopes that Tamate himself had. This friend had been with him for a year, and had been like a son to him in his sorrow. He went with him on this voyage. Besides these two, there were on board Hiro a teacher, Naragi a chief, ten boys who were in training, and the captain.

When the *Nieu* came to the island, she anchored near the village of Dopima. When the villagers saw the ship, they ran down to the shore and tumbled into their canoes. In a very short time the *Nieu* had canoes lying all round her, and natives were climbing up her sides. No one could say how many of them there were. Savages had often come on board when Tamate's ship lay at anchor, but these seemed to be more wilful and fierce than most of the others had been.

At last, as the sun went down behind the island on which their village stood, Tamate ordered them to go home, and said that if they went at once he would land at Dopima and see them next day.

They went away, but when the morning came they would not wait till he could keep his promise. At five o'clock their canoes crossed the water to the *Nieu*. There were many more of the villagers than there had been on the evening of the day before. The deck was so crowded that the men on board could scarcely move about. All around them on their own ship there were dark and angry faces, and in their ears was the clamour of excited voices.

It was not a peaceful welcome that the canoes had brought. They were full of bows and arrows, clubs and spears. Tamate bade the natives begone, but they would not. Then he thought that if he went himself, although it was so early, they would follow him.

He left the Rarotongan teacher with the captain in the *Nieu*. He wished his young friend to stay too. He did not wish him to risk his life, because he hoped that he would live a long time, and carry on the work that he himself had begun. The two men looked at each other. They knew there was great danger. They had seen the hatred and bitterness in the faces of the wild men around them. But Tamate had said he would go. He had never failed to keep his promise to the men and women he sought to help. He would not do it now. And his friend would never let him go alone with that wild mob. The two men stepped into the boat together. The chief and the ten boys joined them, and they rowed for the shore.

The splash of the oars sounded faintly through the shrill shouts of the natives. But Tamate's clear voice rang over all the noise. "Back in half-an-hour to breakfast."

A rush of canoes followed the boat. But those in her looked anxious when they saw how many canoes stayed by the *Nieu*. What could two men do if the natives tried to take the ship?

When the boat reached Dopima the two white men

and some of the boys landed and went to the great club-house. It was the place where all the fighting men met. The other boys stayed to take care of the boat, but soon villagers came to tell them that they too must come to the clubhouse to eat. To feast together is a sign of peace. Tamate was never willing to refuse to eat with the natives. His boys knew this, and left the boat by the shore.

As they feasted in the clubhouse a crash was heard. Naragi and the boys who had come from Daru sprang up. Before them Tamate and his young friend lay dead.

None of them had noticed two armed men who crept along the floor behind the white men till with two blows from their great stone clubs they killed them both.

No one had ever been able to look in Tamate's face and still be angry with him. But from behind a native had had courage to strike him. His eyes could not awe the savage then.

He lay dead. His boys had no hope of escape. One by one they fell beside their master. Naragi fought for his life. He had no weapons, but when he saw the white men fall, he leapt forward and seized another man's club. But one man could not stand long against all those howling warriors, and soon he too lay quiet and still.

The men from the clubhouse went down in triumph to the shore to welcome the others who had stayed by the ship. Their canoes, which had shown only weapons, were now piled high with everything that could be lifted from the *Nieu*. The savages danced and shouted on the beach as they saw the things that had come from the white man's ship. The men were smeared with war paint, and the clothes and books that had been on the *Nieu* were soon stained all over as one wild man after another pounced on what he liked best.

After a time they began to tire of turning over the treasures. A shout rose: "Let us break the boat!"

They scampered off to the creek where the boys had left her. Smash! bang! crash! the stone clubs fell on the beautiful boat. She was the last gift that Mrs. Chalmers had given to the work her husband loved. Crack! crick! went the wood. In a few minutes there was only a pile of splinters. Each warrior took one. Afterwards he stuck it up in his clubhouse to show that he too had had a share in the death of the great white chief.

On board the *Nieu* the captain and Hiro had sent hurried glances after the boat as she went towards the shore. They could not look for long at a time, for they had to try to keep the natives from breaking and wrecking the ship. They saw the boat grow smaller and smaller. They saw the canoes close in upon it. Still they could trace its course. They saw it reach the village and go close to the shore. Then it came out into deep water again. Again it entered the village, and after that they could not see it any more.

No clear sounds came to them from Dopima, but around them were many sounds. Everything that could be taken was seized and thrown into the canoes. It was hard to see good things broken and soiled. But the pain

No boat came

of that was nothing to the pain that Hiro and the captain felt as the hours went on and no signal reached them from the shore.

At last the savages left them and quiet settled down on the ship. The quiet was more dreadful than the noise of the morning had been. It left time to look and look towards the shore for the boat that would never come again.

The *Nieu* lifted her anchor and steamed up and down. All day long she waited near Dopima. After sunset she sailed out to sea beyond the island and anchored there. Next day she sailed along the shore again. The two sad men on board gazed towards the village but no boat came.

At last they sailed to Daru to tell that the great white chief had died for his people.

Yet Tamate did not wish his friends to think of him as dead, when they could not see him any more. He wished them to know that he lives and works gladly in the great life beyond the grave, and that he knows and loves his Master Jesus Christ far better than he could on earth. Not very long before he died, he had written of the life after death, "I shall have good work to do, great brave work for Christ."

As the news of Tamate's death came to Daru, and Motu-motu, Port Moresby and Suau, and to all the villages between them, New Guinea was stricken with sorrow. Men and women and children were sick with grief.

Then the love they had for Tamate brought a new

strength. They wished to do more for the work for which he died than they had ever done before.

There was one old man called Rua. His hands were weak but his heart was strong. It was so good and strong that though it had loved Tamate with passion, it did not hate the men who had killed him.

Rua sat and mourned. His heart knew the thoughts of the white chief's heart. Tamate had longed to win the love of the wild men of Dopima for Jesus Christ. He had died for this. Would his death be in vain? No, it must not be! It might be that Rua could help. He might live for the people for whom his friend had died. The thought fired him. He wrote:

"May you have life and happiness. At this time our hearts are very sad. Tamate and the boys are not here. We shall not see them again. I have wept much. My father Tamate's body I shall not see again, but his spirit we shall certainly see in heaven, if we are strong to do the work of God, thoroughly and all the time. Hear my wish. It is a great wish. My strength I would spend in the place where he was killed. In that village I would live. In that place where they killed men, Jesus Christ's name and His word I would teach to the people, that they may become Jesus' children. My wish is just this. You know it. I have spoken."

Rua could not go to Dopima. A greater joy came to him. Instead of going there to live for Christ and for his friend, he went on a longer journey, to be with Christ and with his friend.

In the clubhouses round Dopima the warriors had stuck up pieces of the broken boat. They pointed to them at their feasts as the signs of their great victory over the white chief and his power.

But in Dopima and all over New Guinea, the death that had seemed to give them the victory was in truth a triumph for the army of Christ. Weak hearts grew brave at the thought of it. Men and women came forward to fight for the Hero whom Tamate had followed even unto death, Jesus Christ, who died for those who hated Him, because He loved them.